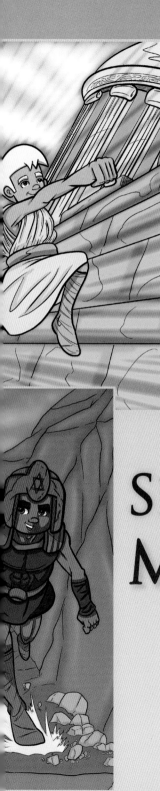

SHIELD OF THE MACCABEES

WRITTEN BY
ERIC A. KIMMEL

ART BY
DOV SMILEY

LETTERED BY   ROD OLLERENSHAW
COVER BY   DOV SMILEY

To Catriella
— **EAK**

To my students, both in-person and virtual
— **DRS**

Apples & Honey Press
An Imprint of Behrman House Publishers
Millburn, New Jersey 07041
www.applesandhoneypress.com

Editorial Consultant: Malka Z. Simkovich, Crown-Ryan Chair of Jewish Studies,
Catholic Theological Union

ISBN 978-1-68115-571-5

Library of Congress Cataloging-in-Publication Data
Names: Kimmel, Eric A., author. | Smiley, Dov, author, illustrator.
Title: Shield of the Maccabees / by Eric A. Kimmel and Dov Smiley;
illustrated by Dov Smiley.
Description: Millburn, New Jersey : Apples and Honey Press, [2021] |
Audience: Grades 4-6. | Summary: "During the time period of the Hanukkah
story, two boys, one Jewish and one Greek, form a lasting friendship"--
Provided by publisher.
Identifiers: LCCN 2020042159 | ISBN 9781681155715 (hardback)
Subjects: LCSH: Graphic novels. | CYAC: Graphic novels. |
Toleration--Fiction. | Jews--History--586 B.C.-70 A.D.--Fiction. |
Greeks--Isreal--Fiction. | War--Fiction. | Hanukkah--Fiction.
Classification: LCC PZ7.7.K575 Sh 2021 | DDC 741.5/973--dc23
LC record available at https://lccn.loc.gov/2020042159

Design by Dov Smiley
Edited by Ann Koffsky
Lettering by Rod Ollerenshaw
Printed in China
9 8 7 6 5 4 3 2 1

IN THE YEAR 351 BCE **ALEXANDER THE GREAT** CREATED A NEW KIND OF EMPIRE.

HE OPENED THE DOORS TO THE RULING **GREEK** CULTURE AND INVITED PEOPLE OF ALL NATIONS TO JOIN IN.

NO MATTER WHO YOU WERE, IF YOU LEARNED TO SPEAK GREEK, DRESSED AS A GREEK, FOLLOWED GREEK CUSTOMS, AND WORSHIPPED GREEK GODS, YOU TOO COULD **BECOME** A GREEK.

BUT NOT EVERYONE APPRECIATED THIS GIFT. IN JUDEA, LAND OF THE JEWS (NOW KNOWN AS **ISRAEL**), MANY OF THE JEWISH PEOPLE HAD DOUBTS.

THE GREEKS CERTAINLY HAD MUCH TO OFFER...

BUT MANY OF THE PEOPLE OF ISRAEL WERE NOT COMFORTABLE WITH HOW MUCH THEIR NEW RULERS WANTED THEM TO **CHANGE**.

GIVING UP THEIR CUSTOMS, THEIR IDENTITY, AND THE RELIGION OF THEIR ANCESTORS SEEMED TOO GREAT A PRICE TO PAY.

IF FORCED TO DO THAT, THEY WOULD **FIGHT**.

OUR STORY BEGINS AT THE TIME OF THE FIRST **HANUKKAH**.

IT STARTS WITH **JASON AND JONATHAN**, TWO BOYS FROM THE COASTAL TOWN OF **SEBASTE** IN THE PROVINCE OF JUDEA.

THEY LIVE IN **DIFFERENT** COMMUNITIES, JEWISH AND GREEK.

THEY DON'T **KNOW** EACH OTHER YET. BUT THEY ARE ABOUT TO BECOME BEST FRIENDS.

AND THEY WILL PLAY A PART IN SOMETHING WE NOW CALL A **MIRACLE**.

ONE MORNING IN THE TOWN OF SEBASTE...

JASON! WAKE UP!

YOU'LL BE LATE FOR SCHOOL AGAIN!

YOW!

WHY DID YOU LET ME SLEEP SO LONG, MOM?

THAT'S RIGHT, BLAME ME.

AT LEAST HAVE SOME BREAKFAST.

DON'T HAVE TIME!

9

LET'S GET OUT OF HERE!

AND DON'T COME BACK!

THAT WAS SOME THROW! WHERE DID YOU LEARN HOW TO DO THAT?

16

YOU SPEAK GREEK WELL, JONATHAN.

I UNDERSTAND COMMON, EVERYDAY GREEK.

HERE WE STUDY *LITERARY* GREEK.

I AM WORRIED YOU MIGHT NOT KNOW ENOUGH FOR THAT.

I REALLY WANT TO STAY...

YOU KNOW...

WE WORK IN *PAIRS* IN MY JEWISH SCHOOL.

THAT WAY WE LEARN FROM EACH OTHER.

FOR THE FIRST LESSON...

CAN JASON BE MY PARTNER?

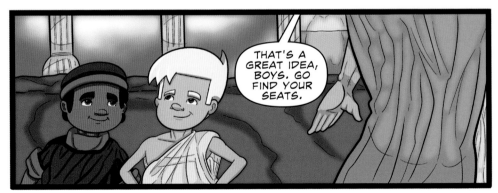

THAT'S A GREAT IDEA, BOYS. GO FIND YOUR SEATS.

21

THE *TRICK* IS, DON'T HOLD IT TOO LONG! IT *WANTS* TO FLY!

YOU GOTTA GIVE IT ONE OF *THESE*!

GO, PEGASUS! *FLY*!

CRASH!!!!

OVER TIME, JASON AND JONATHAN'S FRIENDSHIP GREW.

23

24

IF THERE WAS A FUN ADVENTURE TO BE HAD IN SEBASTE...

...JASON AND JONATHAN WOULD FIND IT *TOGETHER*.

A FEW WEEKS LATER...

HEY, JONATHAN, I GOT YOU SOMETHING!

TA-DA!

I FOUND YOU A SCHOOL TUNIC. NOW YOU'LL BE JUST LIKE THE **REST OF US!**

OH... JASON, I...

I MEAN... THANKS, BUT...

I'M **NOT** GONNA WEAR THAT!

WHAT? I JUST THOUGHT...

YOU KNOW THIS IS A **FORMAL** GREEK TUNIC, RIGHT?

I **REALLY** LIKE GOING TO SCHOOL WITH YOU, JASON.

AND DOING STUFF WITH YOU AFTER SCHOOL IS EVEN **BETTER.**

BUT YOU KNOW THAT I'M NOT GOING TO **TURN** GREEK, RIGHT?

I'M JEWISH AND *PROUD* OF THAT.

I'M NOT GOING TO *CHANGE* WHO I AM OR WHAT I LOOK LIKE.

AND YOU KNOW...SOMETIMES THE GREEKS *FORGET* THAT WE'VE BEEN IN THIS COUNTRY SINCE THE TIME OF *MOSES!*

MAYBE *YOUR* PEOPLE SHOULD BE LEARNING FROM US.

I KNOW THAT I *STAND OUT* FROM YOU AND YOUR OTHER FRIENDS...BUT...

OH! OH, THAT'S *OKAY!*

FORGET I EVEN BROUGHT IT UP!

STAND OUT AND BE YOU! IT'S WHAT I LIKE ABOUT YOU!

YOU SURE, JASON?

ALWAYS, JONATHAN! ALWAYS!

AND WITH THAT, THE BOYS WENT OFF TO THEIR LESSON.

ONE MORE TRY? WHO KNOWS WHAT A CYCLOPS IS?

I THINK I KNOW.

A CYCLOPS IS A MAN WITH ONE EYE.

HOW DO YOU KNOW THAT?

THERE'S A MAN ON OUR STREET. HE WAS A SOLDIER AND LOST AN EYE FIGHTING IN GREECE.

WE ALL CALL HIM SIMON THE *CYCLOPS!*

CLOSE ENOUGH! WELL DONE, JONATHAN!

A CYCLOPS IS *MORE* THAN A MAN.

IT'S A *GIANT* WITH ONE EYE IN THE *MIDDLE* OF HIS FORE-HEAD.

I CAN'T TELL THE STORY AS WELL AS OUR GREAT POET, *HOMER*...

BUT I'LL DO MY BEST TO SHARE IT WITH YOU.

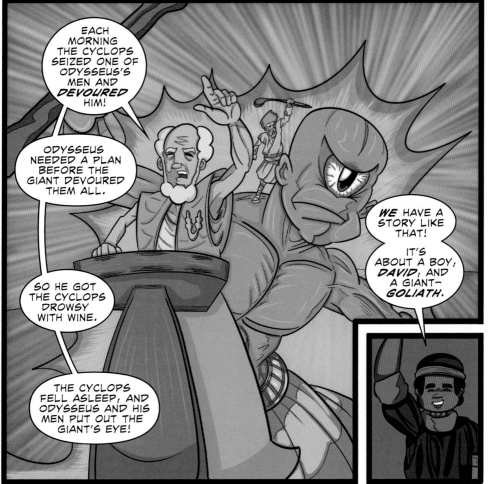

EACH MORNING THE CYCLOPS SEIZED ONE OF ODYSSEUS'S MEN AND *DEVOURED* HIM!

ODYSSEUS NEEDED A PLAN BEFORE THE GIANT DEVOURED THEM ALL.

SO HE GOT THE CYCLOPS DROWSY WITH WINE.

THE CYCLOPS FELL ASLEEP, AND ODYSSEUS AND HIS MEN PUT OUT THE GIANT'S EYE!

WE HAVE A STORY LIKE THAT!

IT'S ABOUT A BOY, *DAVID*, AND A GIANT— *GOLIATH.*

DAVID SLUNG A STONE AT GOLIATH'S FOREHEAD!

DOWN WENT THE GIANT! DAVID WON THE VICTORY AND *SAVED* OUR PEOPLE.

GREAT STORY!

AWESOME!

GOT ANY MORE?

THANK YOU FOR SHARING, JONATHAN. REMEMBER, STUDENTS...

YOU MAY BE POWERLESS... BUT IF YOU USE YOUR BRAINS LIKE DAVID AND ODYSSEUS...YOU'LL *ALWAYS WIN!*

AND DON'T FORGET, WHETHER YOU'RE GREEK OR JEWISH...

EVERYONE HAS A STORY TO TELL.

IT'S ALL WORTH IT. I LIKE STUDYING TORAH AND THE HOLY BOOKS. I LIKE WORKING AS *PARTNERS* WHEN WE READ HERE.

AND I *LOVE* THAT THEY GIVE US DATES AND HONEY IF WE WORK HARD!

GREETINGS. CAN I *JOIN* YOUR GROUP TONIGHT, BOYS?

IT'S *ELAZAR*, THE GREAT JEWISH WARRIOR!

SHOULDN'T YOU BE PROTECTING OUR PEOPLE FROM BANDITS AND RAIDERS?

STUDYING OUR ANCIENT STORIES MAKES ME A *BETTER* FIGHTER, JONATHAN.

IT HELPS ME *REMEMBER* WHAT I'M FIGHTING FOR.

I HOPE YOU'RE READY TO TAKE ON A *GIANT FISH*, BECAUSE THAT'S TONIGHT'S STORY!

FISHING WAS SOMETHING BOTH BOYS LIKED TO DO...

HEY, JONATHAN, WHY DO YOU GO TO THAT GREEK SCHOOL?

ARE YOU STUDYING TO BECOME A GREEK?

KNOWLEDGE ISN'T JEWISH OR GREEK.

AND I'M STUDYING TO BECOME A HUMAN BEING.

A *THINKING HUMAN* BEING!

WE JEWS SPEAK ARAMAIC. THAT'S THE LANGUAGE OF THE *EAST.*

GREEK IS THE LANGUAGE OF THE *WEST.*

IF I KNOW ARAMAIC AND GREEK, I CAN GO *ANYWHERE.*

I STILL DON'T GET WHY YOU DON'T LIKE SCHOOL, JASON.

I LIKE IT FINE, I JUST DON'T THINK THAT WE NEED TO COME EVERY DAY.

YOU LIKE TO SIT AND STUDY. I CAN THINK OF BETTER THINGS TO DO.

YES! THE *ODYSSEY* IS FULL OF GREAT STORIES!

AND IF YOU READ THEM AT HOME, YOU'D KNOW THEM AS WELL AS JONATHAN DOES!!

SO, WHAT DO YOU WANT TO DO TONIGHT?

I DON'T WANT TO READ THE *ODYSSEY*.

WELL, WHY DON'T YOU COME OVER TO MY HOUSE THIS TIME?

PURIM ISN'T AN OFFICIAL HOLIDAY YET.

BUT IT *WILL* BE!

WE CELEBRATE AN EVENT THAT HAPPENED TO US 300 YEARS AGO.

WOW! EVERYONE'S SO EXCITED!

WHAT ARE WE READING AGAIN?

WE'LL READ THE STORY OF ESTHER AND HOW SHE *SAVED* OUR PEOPLE.

NOT EVERYONE APPROVED OF JONATHAN AND JASON'S FRIENDSHIP.

I THINK YOUR SON SPENDS TOO MUCH TIME WITH THAT GREEK BOY.

I THINK YOUR SON SPENDS TOO MUCH TIME WITH THAT JEWISH BOY.

EVENTUALLY, PEOPLE'S WHISPERS MADE IT TO THE BOYS' EARS.

ONE WORLD.

THIS ONE.

AND THE JEWS, YOUR PEOPLE, BELIEVE THAT GOD IS *PERFECT*?

OF COURSE GOD IS! THAT'S WHY GOD IS GOD!

THEN MAY I *CHALLENGE* YOU:

IF GOD IS PERFECT, WHY DID GOD MAKE SUCH AN *IMPERFECT* WORLD?

I DON'T UNDER-STAND.

LOOK AROUND YOU. THIS WORLD IS FULL OF MISERY. WAR, PLAGUE, AND FAMINE. THERE'S A SLAVE MARKET ONLY A SHORT WALK FROM HERE.

WHY WOULD A PERFECT GOD *CREATE* SUCH THINGS?

I DON'T KNOW.

I NEVER THOUGHT ABOUT THAT.

WHAT'S THE ANSWER?

46

I DON'T KNOW EITHER!

BUT YOU'RE THE TEACHER. AREN'T YOU SUPPOSED TO KNOW?

NO...

"I'M SUPPOSED TO ASK QUESTIONS.

"PLATO'S TEACHER, SOCRATES, TAUGHT US THAT.

"IF WE KEEP ASKING THE RIGHT QUESTIONS...

"SOONER OR LATER...

WE WILL ARRIVE AT THE TRUTH.

47

ONE HOT SUMMER AFTERNOON...

IT'S HOT! I'M MELTING.

I WISH THERE WAS SOMETHING TO DO.

ME TOO!

HOW ABOUT GOING SWIMMING?

TOO CROWDED! EVERYONE IN TOWN IS AT THE BEACH.

THAT NEW *ARISTOPHANES* PLAY IS AT THE AMPHITHEATER.

WE CAN'T GET IN WITHOUT AN ADULT.

I GIVE UP. WHAT DO YOU WANT TO DO?

I KNOW! LET'S LOOK FOR *TREASURE!*

WHERE? *HERE* IN SEBASTE?

NO. IN THE HILLS. THERE ARE ALL KINDS OF *CAVES* UP THERE.

WE'RE SURE TO FIND SOMETHING, LET'S GO!

THEY HIKED... AND HIKED...

AND HIKED...

WE'RE ALMOST THERE.

EVENTUALLY, THE BOYS FOUND A CAVE.

THINK WE'LL FIND KING SOLOMON'S TREASURE?

I'LL SETTLE FOR ALEXANDER THE GREAT'S SWEATY SANDALS!

HEY! I FOUND SOMETHING!

WHAT IS IT?

AN IDOL! PUT IT BACK, JASON! COVER IT UP!

WHY ARE YOU SO FRIGHTENED? IT'S JUST A STATUE.

IT'S AN IDOL. I DON'T EVEN WANT TO LOOK AT IT!

YOUR LAND? HOLD ON! I LIVE HERE, TOO!

THIS IS MY COUNTRY AS MUCH AS YOURS!

I KNOW GREEKS WHO SAY JEWS DON'T BELONG HERE. I NEVER THOUGHT *YOU* WOULD FEEL THAT WAY ABOUT *US!*

YOU DON'T KNOW WHAT IT'S LIKE TO BE *CONQUERED!*

WE WILL *NEVER* GIVE UP OUR RELIGION.

WHAT?

DO YOU REALLY THINK WE WOULD *FORCE* YOU TO DO THAT?

I DON'T... I DIDN'T MEAN...

LOOK! THE IDOL IS MAKING *TROUBLE.*

IT'S NOT MAKING TROUBLE!

IT'S NOT DOING ANYTHING!

IT'S ONLY A STATUE!

THEN WHY ARE WE *YELLING* AT EACH OTHER?!

THEY JUST COULD NOT PUT IT BEHIND THEM...

LOOK, I DON'T WANT TO MAKE THIS A BIG DEAL, JONATHAN...

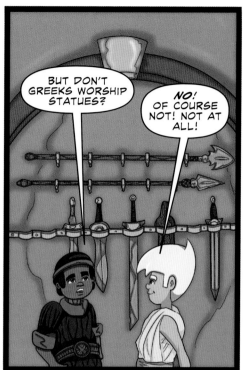

BUT DON'T GREEKS WORSHIP STATUES?

NO! OF COURSE NOT! NOT AT ALL!

WE WORSHIP THE *GODS.*

WHAT'S THE DIFFERENCE?

OH, BOY, HOW WOULD MASTER APOLLONIUS EXPLAIN IT?

THEY ARGUED FOR TWO DAYS...

53

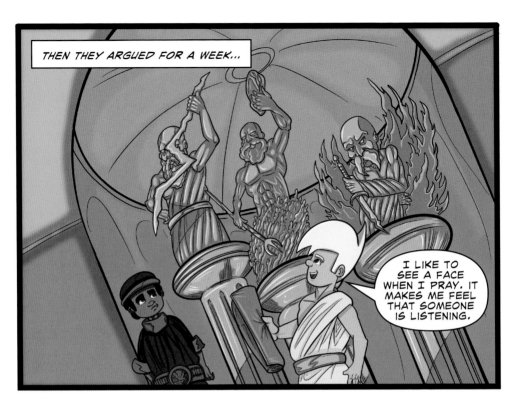

THEN THEY ARGUED FOR A WEEK...

I LIKE TO SEE A FACE WHEN I PRAY. IT MAKES ME FEEL THAT SOMEONE IS LISTENING.

TRY THIS. THE IMAGE OF OUR KING, *ANTIOCHUS*, IS ON THIS COIN. DOES ANYONE—JEWISH OR GREEK—THINK THIS COIN IS OUR RULER?

NO WAY! ESPECIALLY THAT FACE!

IT'S THE SAME WITH STATUES, THE IMAGES OF THE GODS. THEY GUIDE OUR PRAYERS.

AND ANOTHER WEEK...

I CAN UNDERSTAND THAT. BUT WHY DO YOU NEED SO MANY GODS?

I THINK IT'S BECAUSE PEOPLE HAVE DIFFERENT NEEDS AT DIFFERENT TIMES.

IF I NEED A POWERFUL FRIEND, I'LL PRAY TO ZEUS. HE'S KING OF THE GODS.

IF I NEED COMFORT, I'LL PRAY TO HERA, THE HEAVENLY MOTHER.

IF I WANT A GIRL TO LIKE ME, I'LL CALL ON APHRODITE, THE GODDESS OF *LOVE*.

SOME PEOPLE JUST LIKE ONE GOD BETTER THAN OTHERS. DO YOU SEE NOW?

WE DON'T WORSHIP STATUES. WE WORSHIP *IDEAS*.

IT DOES TO US.

GOD IS LIKE THE WIND.

YOU *CAN'T* SEE IT.

BUT YOU *FEEL* IT. YOU KNOW IT'S THERE.

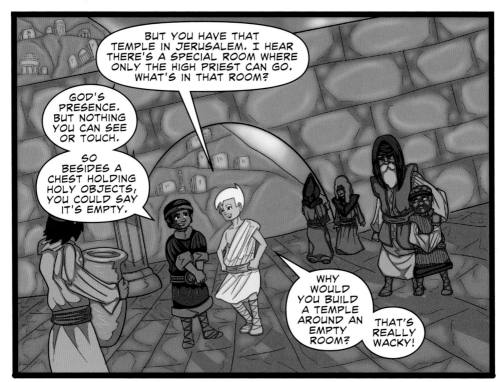

BUT YOU HAVE THAT TEMPLE IN JERUSALEM. I HEAR THERE'S A SPECIAL ROOM WHERE ONLY THE HIGH PRIEST CAN GO. WHAT'S IN THAT ROOM?

GOD'S PRESENCE. BUT NOTHING YOU CAN SEE OR TOUCH.

SO BESIDES A CHEST HOLDING HOLY OBJECTS, YOU COULD SAY IT'S EMPTY.

WHY WOULD YOU BUILD A TEMPLE AROUND AN EMPTY ROOM?

THAT'S REALLY WACKY!

IN THE PALACE OF KING ANTIOCHUS IV.

THE KING IS FREE AT LAST, BUT WE HAD TO PAY A HUGE RANSOM!

ANTIOCHUS IS *CRAZY!*

CRAZIER THAN HE WAS *BEFORE* HE LOST A WAR TO KING PTOLEMY?

WE SHOULD HAVE *LEFT* HIM IN EGYPT.

WHO KNOWS HOW HORRIBLE ANTIOCHUS WILL BE, NOW THAT HE IS *HUMILIATED!*

MY ARMY IS DESTROYED. SOMEONE BETRAYED ME. NOW I KNOW WHO!

SLAM!

WHO, KING ANTIOCHUS?

THE *JEWS!!!*

64

SOON AFTER THAT, A NOTICE APPEARED IN THE MARKETPLACE.

WHAT DOES IT SAY?

THAT'S STRANGE.

KING ANTIOCHUS DECREES THAT ALL LOYAL SUBJECTS MUST BECOME *GREEKS*.

WORSHIPPING THE JEWISH GOD, CELEBRATING JEWISH HOLIDAYS, STUDYING JEWISH TEXTS, AND FOLLOWING JEWISH LAWS AND CUSTOMS ARE *FORBIDDEN*.

THOSE REFUSING TO WORSHIP THE GREEK GODS WILL BE PUT TO DEATH!

ONE NATION, ONE PEOPLE, ONE SET OF GODS?

LOVE IT OR LEAVE IT?

THERE'S GONNA BE TROUBLE.

SOME THOUGHT THE NEW LAW WAS A GOOD IDEA.

OTHERS DID NOT.

HOW CAN YOU FORCE PEOPLE TO WORSHIP GODS THEY DON'T BELIEVE IN?

KING ALEXANDER LET US WORSHIP AS WE PLEASED.

HE NEVER FORCED ANYONE TO WORSHIP HIS WAY.

WHAT DO YOU THINK, MASTER APOLLONIUS?

FOOLISH AND DANGEROUS.

OUR MASTER SOCRATES TAUGHT THAT TRUTH MUST BE DISCOVERED, NOT DECREED. HE CHALLENGED THE RULERS WITH HIS QUESTIONS.

SO THEY KILLED HIM.

MADNESS LIKE THIS WILL LEAD TO WAR AND PAIN FOR US ALL!

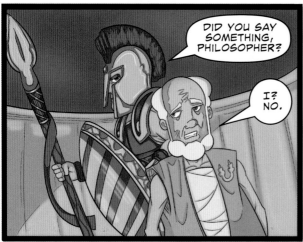

DID YOU SAY SOMETHING, PHILOSOPHER?

I? NO.

NOTHING.

TROUBLE WAS NOT LONG IN COMING.

ONE DAY, IN THE TOWN OF MODI'IN... EVERYTHING CHANGED.

COME, JEWS! SHOW YOUR LOYALTY TO OUR KING!

WHO WILL BE FIRST TO OFFER SACRIFICE?

TRAITORS!

BECOME GREEK OR MEET YOUR END!

THINGS HAVE GONE CRAZY!

HOW DARE THEY!!!

SOON, SOME JEWS CHOSE TO SIDE WITH THE GREEKS...

BY BECOMING A GREEK, I PROVE MY LOYALTY TO MY KING.

AND SO WILL YOU!

THE FIRE OF WAR WAS LIT ALL OVER THE COUNTRY...

THERE WAS NO PUTTING IT OUT.

FOLLOW ME, JONATHAN!

WHERE ARE YOU TAKING ME, DAD?

MOM! STOP PULLING!

IT'S NOT SAFE HERE, JASON!

THE BOYS STAYED WHERE THEY WERE TOLD.

YOU NEED TO HIDE HERE, JASON.

DON'T COME OUT UNTIL IT'S SAFE, JONATHAN.

THEY STAYED ALONE AND HIDDEN.

AS THEY WAITED, THE VIOLENCE OUTSIDE THEIR HIDING PLACES ONLY GOT WORSE.

IT WAS TERRIFYING.

WAITING ALONE.

HOPING THE PEOPLE THEY LOVED WERE SAFE.

ALL THE WHILE THEY EACH HEARD SHOUTS AND SCREAMS.

SOON, ALL THEY COULD FEEL WERE...

ANGER

FEAR

HATRED

MADNESS

IT TORE THROUGH THE COUNTRY.

VIOLENCE SPREAD ACROSS THE LAND.

CITY FOUGHT CITY.

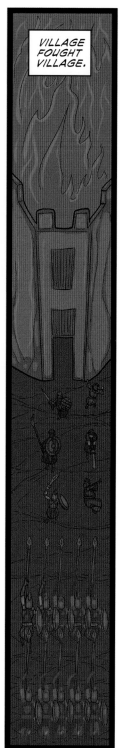

VILLAGE FOUGHT VILLAGE.

NEIGHBOR FOUGHT NEIGHBOR.

AND SEBASTE WAS NOT SPARED.

AT LAST...SILENCE.

MASTER APOLLONIUS! WHAT HAPPENED?

THEY BURNED OUR LIBRARY.

WHY?

WHY WOULD ANYONE FEAR KNOWLEDGE?

THEY USED THE TORAH SCROLLS TO SET FIRE TO OUR HOUSE OF PRAYER.

BUT WHY, ELAZAR?

WHY? ASK KING ANTIOCHUS. ASK HIS SOLDIERS. ASK THE TRAITORS WHO DO HIS DIRTY WORK...

AS THEY VOWED VENGEANCE, THEIR COUNTRY WENT TO WAR WITH ITSELF.

JASON JOINED THE GREEK ARMY...

AND JONATHAN SWORE AN OATH TO THE MACCABEES.

MONTHS PASSED...

LISTEN UP, YOU SLACKERS! LISTEN **GOOD!**

"IF YOU WANT TO STAY **ALIVE** IN BATTLE, YOU HAVE TO DRILL, DRILL, **DRILL!**

"JEWS ARE SOME OF THE BEST SOLDIERS IN THE **WORLD.**

THEY'RE HIRED AS MERCENARIES EVERYWHERE.

EMPIRES WOULDN'T BE PAYING THEM BIG BUCKS IF THEY DIDN'T KNOW THEIR JOB...

SO YOU'D BETTER KNOW **YOURS!**

DO IT AGAIN!

GET IT RIGHT THIS TIME!

OVERLAP SHIELDS!

SPEARS READY!

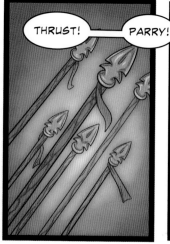

THRUST!

PARRY!

RECOVER!

80

THE GREEKS ARE THE BEST SOLDIERS IN THE WORLD.

NEVER UNDERESTIMATE THEM.

I'VE FOUGHT WITH GREEKS.

AND AGAINST GREEKS.

THEY CAN BE *BEATEN.*

GREEKS FIGHT IN A *PHALANX.* THAT'S A TIGHT FORMATION OF SPEARMEN.

"IF WE BREAK THE *PHALANX,* WE WIN!

HOW DO WE DO IT?

FIGHT FROM A DISTANCE WITH ARROWS AND SLINGS.

USE THE TERRAIN. FIGHT ON OUR HILLS OR BROKEN GROUND.

MAKE THE GREEKS FIGHT *OUR* WAR.

YOU FIRST, JONATHAN.

SHOW ME HOW TO USE A SWORD AGAINST A SPEAR.

81

GET IN CLOSE.

THRUST!

PARRY!

RECOVER!

THE BOYS TRAIN HARD.

AFTER FIVE MONTHS OF TRAINING...

THEY ARE READY FOR BATTLE.

THE RECRUITS ARE GIVEN THEIR FIRST ORDERS.

THE GREEKS LEARN THAT THE JEWISH REBELS ARE HIDING IN A VALLEY.

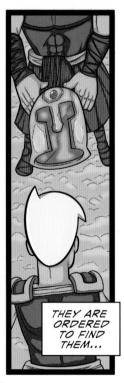

THEY ARE ORDERED TO FIND THEM...

AND DESTROY THEM.

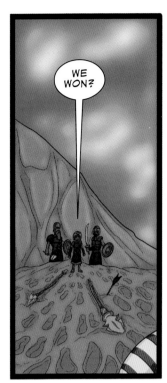

88

BECAUSE THEY'RE NOT FIGHTING YOUR *BEST* SOLDIERS.

YOUR BEST SOLDIERS ARE BATTLING EGYPT AND ROME. YOU'RE FIGHTING THE JEWS WITH WHAT'S *LEFT.*

HALF-TRAINED RECRUITS, THIRD-RATE GENERALS, AND *MERCENARIES.*

THE JEWS ARE FIGHTING FOR THEIR GOD AND RELIGION.

MOST OF OUR TROOPS ARE FIGHTING FOR *PAY.*

91

92

"THIS IS A FIGHT FOR THE *FUTURE*!

"ONLY ONE OF OUR CULTURES CAN *EXIST* ON THIS EARTH. GREECE OR ISRAEL.

"FUTURE GENERATIONS WILL REMEMBER THE MIGHT OF *KING ANTIOCHUS*!

"ALL THEY WILL REMEMBER OF THE JEWS IS HOW EASILY I *DEFEATED* THEM!

MEANWHILE...

YOUR ORDERS ARE TO GUARD THIS CAVE, JASON.

INSIDE IS THE SACRED OIL WE TOOK FROM THE JEWISH TEMPLE.

THEY NEED IT TO LIGHT A BIG GOLDEN LAMP.

WE'LL HIDE IT HERE.

NO OIL MEANS NO GOD.

THEY'LL *HAVE* TO BECOME GREEKS.

WHAT DOES THEIR GOD *LOOK* LIKE?

LIKE US.

HA! I HEAR THEY WORSHIP A GOLDEN CALF.

YOU GUYS DON'T KNOW WHAT YOU'RE TALKING ABOUT.

BY THE GODS, JASON. YOU'RE ALMOST A JEW YOURSELF.

WHAT'S WRONG WITH *THAT?!!*

THEY'RE TOUGH AND BRAVE...

AND BEING GREEK *USED* TO MEAN MORE THAN STARTING POINTLESS WARS!

THEY'RE CRUSHING US, ELAZAR!

WE'RE NO MATCH FOR THESE ANIMALS!

THERE'S *NO WAY* WE CAN WIN!

LISTEN TO ME.

THE KING MUST BE ON THAT ELEPHANT!

ONLY A ROYAL ELEPHANT HAS ARMOR LIKE THAT!

DEFEAT ANTIOCHUS AND WE *END* THE WAR.

NONE OF US MAY COME BACK.

BUT OUR NAMES WILL LIVE FOREVER.

LIKE DAVID, WHO BROUGHT DOWN THE GIANT WITH A *STONE!*

LIKE SAMSON, WHO OVERCAME A LION WITH HIS *BARE HANDS.*

LIKE JOSHUA, WHO TOPPLED THE WALLS OF JERICHO WITH A SHOFAR *BLAST!*

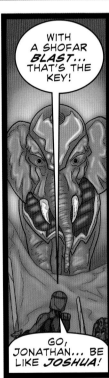

WITH A SHOFAR *BLAST...* THAT'S THE KEY!

GO, JONATHAN... BE LIKE *JOSHUA!*

EVERYONE, *CHARGE!*

GO FOR THE *ELEPHANTS!*

DON'T STOP! KEEP *GOING!*

NOW, JONATHAN! BLOW AS HARD AS YOU *CAN!*

TEKIAH!!!

THE SHOFAR BLAST STARTLED THE ELEPHANT.

TEKIAHHHHHHH!!!

CRASH!

AND IT STAMPEDED... RIGHT THROUGH THE GREEK LINES.

AND ANTIOCHUS'S ULTIMATE WEAPON...

TURNED ON THE GREEKS THEMSELVES.

A VICTORY HAD BEEN WON.

BUT AT A TERRIBLE PRICE.

IT WORKED, ELAZAR!

OH, NO...

THE ELEPHANT TRAMPLED MY COMMANDER TO GET AWAY.

THE KING WAS *NOT* ON THAT ELEPHANT.

ELAZAR'S SACRIFICE WAS FOR *NOTHING.*

GOD HAS *BLESSED* US WITH VICTORY.

A FEW MORE BATTLES AND THE GREEKS WILL BE *GONE.*

OUR PEOPLE WILL BE FREE AGAIN.

YOU CALL THIS A *BLESSING?*

LOOK AROUND. OUR COUNTRY IS WRECKED.

I WAS HAPPY ONCE. THE "ENEMY" WAS MY FRIEND.

MY FRIEND... MOST LIKELY DEAD NOW...

HOW DID IT COME TO THIS?

CHAPTER 8: THE VICTORY

AFTER MORE FIGHTING, THE DAY FINALLY CAME.

THE GREEK ARMY FOUND ITSELF BESIEGED BEHIND THE WALLS OF JERUSALEM.

IT LOOKS AS IF THE WHOLE JEWISH ARMY IS HERE.

DON'T WORRY, JASON...

"THESE WALLS ARE STRONG."

WE CAN HOLD OUT FOR A LONG TIME.

YEAH, I KNOW...

BUT WHAT IF THEY ATTACK *ALL* THE WALLS AT ONCE?

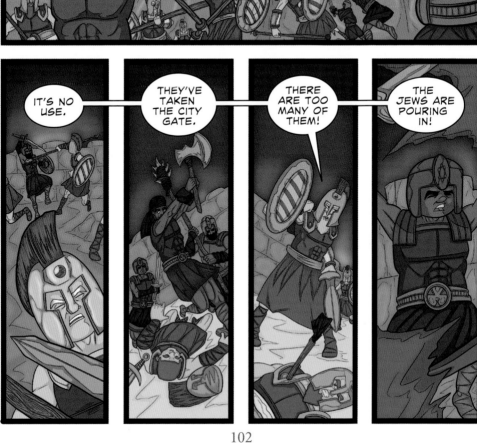

103

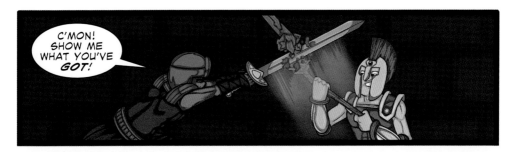

SMASH!!!!

JUST GET UP. I *DON'T* WANT TO HURT YOU.

I'M DONE WITH THIS *STUPID WAR!*

YOU GO YOUR WAY. *I'LL GO MINE...*

HOW DID YOU *DO* THAT?

HOW DO YOU KNOW THAT *THROW?*

MY FRIEND TAUGHT ME. MY BEST FRIEND.

I LEARNED IT LONG AGO.

WHEN THE WORLD MADE *SENSE.*

HOW DID IT COME TO THIS?!!

WHY ARE WE FIGHTING EACH OTHER?

I HAVE NO IDEA. I'VE THOUGHT ABOUT THAT FOR A LONG TIME.

DO YOU REMEMBER THAT STORY FROM PLATO...

THE ONE THAT MASTER APOLLONIUS TOLD US?

OF COURSE! THE STORY OF THE SHADOWS...

I'VE NEVER FORGOTTEN THAT STORY...

THAT STORY EXPLAINS *EVERYTHING*...

WHY WE DO SUCH *HORRIBLE* THINGS...

WE ARE THE PEOPLE IN THE CAVE...

AND WE LIVE IN A *WORLD* OF SHADOWS.

IT'S *DARK* AND *SCARY!*

IT *CAN* BE...

BUT THAT ISN'T THE *REAL* WORLD.

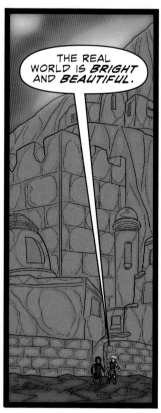

THE REAL WORLD IS *BRIGHT* AND *BEAUTIFUL.*

IT'S THE WORLD GOD MADE.

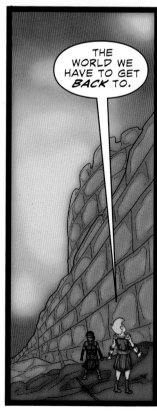

THE WORLD WE HAVE TO GET *BACK* TO.

HOW DO WE DO THAT? THE WAR ISN'T OVER...

AND IF ANY SOLDIERS SEE US...

IF ANYONE SEES US, THEY'LL ORDER US TO *KILL* EACH OTHER.

YOU'RE RIGHT, JASON.

FOR NOW, WE HAVE TO STAY ALIVE.

AND I THINK I HAVE A PLAN.

IT MIGHT WORK... WE'LL STAY TOGETHER...

AND IF ANYONE SEES US, WE'LL *PRETEND* TO BE EACH OTHER'S PRISONER.

TAKE MY SWORD.

IF WE RUN INTO GREEKS, I'LL BE YOUR PRISONER.

I GET IT!

AND IF WE RUN INTO JEWS, I'LL SLIP YOU THE SWORD AND BE *YOUR* PRISONER.

DO YOU TRUST ME WITH YOUR LIFE, JONATHAN?

ALWAYS, JASON.

ALWAYS.

AND SOON ENOUGH...

WE NEED TO PASS THIS BATTALION...

LET ME DO THE TALKING.

HO! WHERE ARE YOU TAKING THAT JEWISH DOG, SOLDIER?

HE'S MY PRISONER. I'M GOING TO SELL HIM TO THE SLAVERS WHEN THIS WAR IS OVER.

YOU SHOULD RUN ALONG TO THE CITADEL BEFORE THEY CLOSE THE GATE.

I'LL TAKE CARE OF THAT PRISONER FOR YOU.

FILTHY IDOL WORSHIPPER!

LET'S *KILL* HIM!

STAND *BACK!* THIS IS AN IMPORTANT PRISONER.

I HAVE ORDERS TO BRING HIM TO JUDAH MACCABEE HIMSELF.

WHO IS HE?

WHY IS HE SO IMPORTANT?

WHY, THIS IS *ODYSSEUS,* SON OF KING CYCLOPS OF TROY!

COUSIN TO KING ANTIOCHUS *HIMSELF!*

OH!

THAT'S DIFFERENT, THEN...

YOU MAY PASS.

KING CYCLOPS OF TROY? WHERE DID THAT—

HOW COULD I FORGET THAT ONE-EYED GIANT!

JASON AND JONATHAN CONTINUED ON...

SOMETIMES THEY RAN INTO GREEKS. SOMETIMES THEY RAN INTO JEWS...

BUT THEY TRUSTED EACH OTHER AND SURVIVED.

CHAPTER 9: THE TEMPLE

SOON, THE JEWS WERE VICTORIOUS.

THEY HAD BEATEN THE GREATEST ARMY ON THE PLANET.

KING ANTIOCHUS NO LONGER RULED THEM.

THE JEWISH PEOPLE HAD WON THE RIGHT TO WORSHIP THEIR OWN WAY. THEY WERE A FREE PEOPLE IN THEIR OWN LAND ONCE MORE.

THE DEFEATED GREEKS HURRIED TO GET TO THE CITADEL FORTRESS.

BUT NOT ALL GREEKS COULD GET THERE IN TIME.

THEY CLOSED THE FORTRESS GATE.

WHERE CAN I GO?

I KNOW. FOLLOW ME.

TO WHERE?

TO THE ONE PLACE YOU'LL BE SAFE.

116

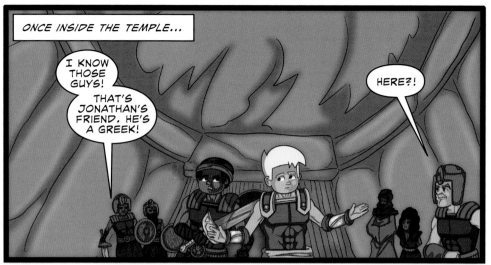

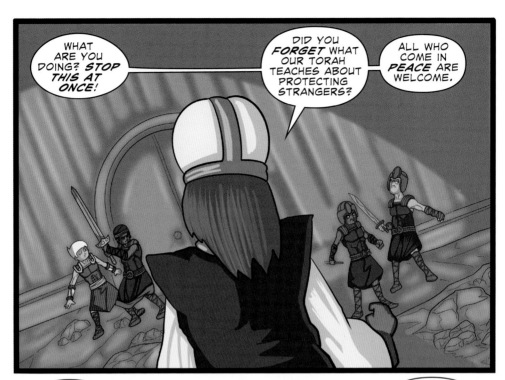

118

AT LAST, AFTER SO MUCH WAR, LET US RE-DEDICATE GOD'S TEMPLE AS BEST WE CAN.

JONATHAN... I MAY BE ABLE TO HELP...

AND AS THE LIGHT CAME BACK INTO THE TEMPLE...

THE PEOPLE PRAYED THAT GOD'S HOLY LIGHT WOULD SHINE ALL OVER THE WORLD.

THE OIL IS IN A CAVE FOUR DAYS JOURNEY FROM HERE.

I KNOW THE WAY THERE.

THE HIGH PRIEST GAVE THE ORDER.

JASON AND JONATHAN LED HIS SERVANTS TO WHERE THE OIL WAS HIDDEN.

THE SERVANTS RETURNED EIGHT DAYS LATER TO FIND THE MENORAH STILL BURNING.

JASON AND JONATHAN DID NOT SEE THE MIRACLE.

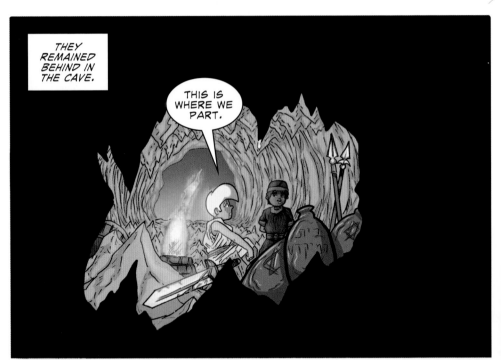

THAT NIGHT, FAR ABOVE THE FORTRESS AND THE TEMPLE MOUNT...

FAR ABOVE THE MOON AND STARS...

UNSEEN GOD, RULER OF HEAVEN AND EARTH, WATCH OVER MY FRIEND...

...PROTECT HIM AND KEEP HIM SAFE UNTIL YOU BRING US BOTH TO A TIME OF PEACE.

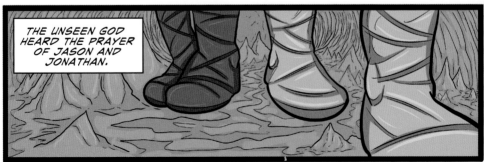

THE UNSEEN GOD HEARD THE PRAYER OF JASON AND JONATHAN.

Author's Note

Hanukkah has always been my favorite Jewish holiday, just as Jewish history has always been my favorite subject. However, as often happens the more I learned, the more I came to realize that I had been missing lots of important facts. There was a lot more to the Hanukkah story than "Good Jews/Bad Greeks/Light candles/Let's eat!"

Jews and Greeks living in Israel two thousand years ago were not mortal enemies. While there was sometimes tension between the two peoples, they learned a lot from each other and got along reasonably well. The Maccabean War was not only the product of racial or religious hatred. It was also sparked by an unstable king trying to hold together an unstable empire by forcing his diverse subjects to adopt a single culture and religion.

Antiochus's campaign of repression and persecution didn't work. Instead of turning Jews into Greeks, it sparked a religious war that led to the creation of an independent Jewish state.

Every war is a tragedy, no matter who wins. That is why, as I light the Hanukkah candles, I recall why I wrote the story of Jason and Jonathan, two friends from long ago who found themselves on opposite sides of a battlefield in a war that didn't have to happen. What can we learn from their story? We learn that—while it is never easy—people of different cultures and religions can always develop mutual respect and understanding if they sincerely make the effort. This is why it is so important to listen—really listen—to one another.

— **Eric A. Kimmel**

The Star of David *(Magen David)* did not become a Jewish symbol until the Middle Ages. No one knows under which symbol the Maccabees fought.

Sebaste is an imaginary town modeled on the port city of Caesarea, whose impressive amphitheater and harbor still stand.

Greek schools *(ephebia)* were reserved for the sons of wealthy Greeks. Jonathan would not have been admitted.

Jonathan would never have entered a **gymnasium**. It would have been too hostile a place for a religious Jew.

- **Elephants** were the tanks of ancient warfare. They often panicked in the midst of battle and charged through their own army's lines.

- **The Temple Menorah** was carried off by the Romans, who destroyed the Temple in 70 CE. No one has reported seeing the original Menorah for fifteen hundred years.

- **Jewish women** might really have fought with the Maccabees. We know that Jewish women defied Antiochus's orders to worship idols; defying the tyrant's command is as much a way of fighting back as taking up a sword.

Eric A. Kimmel is the author of nearly 150 books for children, including the Hanukkah classic *Hershel and the Hanukkah Goblins*. He is a five-time recipient of the National Jewish Book Award as well as having been awarded the Sydney Taylor Lifetime Achievement Award by the Association of Jewish Libraries. *Shield of the Maccabees* is his first graphic novel. He and his wife, Doris, live in Portland, Oregon.

Dov Smiley is an illustrator and a Jewish educator. He has authored and illustrated multiple graphic novels and comic books, including *Jewish Holiday Comics*, *Torah Comics*, and *The Book of Jonah*, all of which are used as educational tools in Jewish schools and synagogues across North America. He lives in Union City, New Jersey.